Jock's Island

by ELIZABETH COATSWORTH

Illustrated by Lilian Obligado

Cover by Mort Künstler

SCHOLASTIC BOOK SERVICES

NEW YORK · TORONTO · LONDON · AUCKLAND · SYDNEY · TOKYO

For
Helen Crosby Hekimian
in memory of old and
pleasant sojourns together

Copyright © 1963 by Elizabeth Coatsworth and Lilian Obligado Simonetti.
This edition is published by Scholastic Book Services, a division of Scholastic Magazines, Inc., by arrangement with The Viking Press, Inc.

15 14 13 12 11 10 9 8 7 6 5 4   7 8 9/7 0 1 2/8

Printed in the U.S.A.   11

There is an island, wrinkled and alone,
   An island in cold seas,
Far from the sirens and the golden shores
   Of the Hesperides.

This island is a fort against the waves,
   Here nothing grows
Luxuriantly. There are no somnolent palms,
   Nor scent of rose.

Only the cold sea strikes against the rock,
   The cold wind screams,
And through the fog, like a small flying bird,
   The cold sun gleams.

Chapter One

THE ISLAND rose out of the sea like the stump of a tree of volcanic rock, rotted away in the centre to the dead crater with its sky-reflecting lake.

On the outer slope of the crater, the land went down steeply to furrowed cliffs rooted in the bottom of the sea, so that neither winds nor waves could shake them.

Only in two or three places, where water had worn the black rock into gullies, could the cliffs be climbed to reach the rough pasture land above, where Old Tom's sheep grazed.

One gully led down to the apron of old lava where the village had its potato fields and cow pas-

tures. At the foot of this path, earlier shepherds had built a sheepfold and hut, and here Old Tom stood now, counting his flock as Jock drove them from the mountain.

Tom had grown so old that he no longer went

up into the high meadows. He was a heavy, bent man, short of stature, short of wind, and short of temper. He had trained Jock harshly, but not so harshly as to break the dog's spirit. Tom seldom praised, but he was just. He and Jock respected each other, even if there was no bond of love between them.

On this morning both man and dog were uneasy. There was a strange smell in the air, and several times in the last few days the mountain had shaken, not with the vibration of the sea but with something stronger and more secret. Worse still, from the direction of the unseen village, a wisp of evil-smelling steam rose, as if a pot of sulphur were boiling over on some giant stove, and with the stench came a curious hissing.

Jock sensed danger without knowing where or what it was. Old Tom knew well enough. Earlier in the week a great puddle of boiling mud had appeared between the village and the nearest cliff. Day by day the thing grew larger and, as the mud cooled and dried, it had built itself higher, bubble by foul bubble. Now it was overflowing, and the hiss came as the hot mud met the sea. At first Old Tom and the rest of the villagers had been only interested in this new appearance, but as the cone rose higher, they became alarmed,

Where would it all end?

Whatever happened, Old Tom had the shearing of his sheep to attend to. So, at the usual time, he sent Jock up into the pastures to bring down the flock, while he waited in the hut by the sheepfold.

Early one cold and windy morning he heard the bleating of the sheep, and, after putting some food in a dish, came out of his shelter with a blanket blowing around his shoulders. He put the dish on the ground, and stood watching the flock slowly making its way down the short zigzags and slides of the trail, with black and white Jock behind it.

As each sheep came to the level land, Tom drove it into the fold, forming a first idea of how it had fared since he had seen it last. Very soon his eye, practiced with years of sheep-counting, saw that two of the thirty-odd ewes were missing.

He turned to Jock, who stood panting at the foot of the trail, his bright, anxious eyes showing that he knew, as well as his master did, that all the flock was not there.

"First eat the food I've brought you, and then go back and fetch the others down," said Old Tom.

"They may be dead for all I can tell, so I can't lambaste you for coming without them, but go back you must while the rest are folded. If they're alive, bring them down, while I get on with the shearing."

Jock ate his food. Hungry as he was, he did not bolt it but took it in a steady workmanlike manner, and, when he had finished, started off up the breakneck trail without waiting for further orders. He was a border collie, coal-black, except for a narrow white streak down his face and a white ruff and paws. Like all border collies, he was wide between the eyes, short-coupled and plumy-tailed, and his feet were small and strongly padded. If Tom and his forefathers had been shepherds for generations, Jock and his ancestors had been sheep dogs for just as long. The care of the flock was bred in his bones. The sheep were his occupation, and their safety was his honour.

Chapter Two

Now Jock was alone on the mountain, trotting slowly but steadily along. He did not follow any trail but went as a hungry fox goes, searching each gully and thicket, his eyes and ears and nose alert. Here the smell of sulphur was weaker, but at first he could not quite rid his nostrils of it. It troubled him, partly because it came between him and the smell of the sheep which he had come to find.

It took several hours to find the first ewe, a lambless creature and a natural runaway. Wherever she had hidden earlier, she had in time grown thirsty and ventured into the hollow crater to drink at the lake which lay at its bottom. There she stood as if about to drink, but she was not drinking. Another curious thing was the circling of the gulls, around and around over the surface of the lake, crying out, but not landing on the water, as was their custom when they wished to rest for a while below the wild sweep of the wind.

Why was the ewe not drinking? Why were the gulls crying? Jock took the thread of path leading down into the crater, slipping and sliding on the lava gravel, his eyes on the sheep, ready to head her off if she tried to scramble up the slope by some other way.

But the ewe never moved. She seemed in a daze of surprise, and the gulls shrieked and circled, circled and shrieked, white against the black sides of the crater. Now, as Jock descended, the air seemed to be growing warmer, and his nose began to twitch in distaste. The strange smell was becoming stronger, and he could see a slight mist rising from the surface of the lake. He, too, was thirsty, but he would not stoop his head to that warm and evil-smelling water which had once been so cold and so clear. The ewe made no attempt to escape him. She seemed glad to see a familiar creature near her and, at his bark, climbed obediently back along the path to the rim.

The second sheep was harder to find. It was an eagle that showed Jock where she was, as again and again the great bird circled and dropped down upon something hidden from view under a thorn bush. At the sight Jock was swept by fury. He drove the ewe he had with him into a thicket, and then, flat on his belly, stalked the eagle. As he drew near, he could make out the bird's quarry, a new-born lamb with its mother standing over it. The ewe was bleeding from repeated slashes of the eagle's talons but still braced herself, striking up as she could with her forefeet at the wings which beat about her.

Neither the eagle nor the ewe was aware of Jock's approach, and the next time the bird swept low Jock sprang on it, his teeth slashing along the nearest wing. The eagle struggled upward, hurt, but able to fly. It swung slowly in a circle overhead, eyeing the lamb and the almost defeated ewe, eyeing this new ally of theirs which had come to their aid so unexpectedly.

Perhaps the bird had never seen a dog before, but it understood that it had met its equal. The lamb was not for it, except at too great a cost. It hung in the air, in case the dog should finish up the lamb himself, for, great and savage as the eagle was, it was not above taking scraps if it could not have the full meal.

But there was no lamb killing. The wounded ewe lay down to rest, and the lamb lay close beside her, while Jock stood near, head raised, a low growl moving the white hairs along his throat as he watched the enemy, ready for some new attack.

All this the eagle saw with an eye which could see a mouse in the grass from the heights of the air. He would have to find his dinner elsewhere. No animal has time for regrets, and away the great bird circled, watching for other prey.

Chapter Three

THE ISLAND was like an enormous tree stump rising straight out of the Atlantic, but on clear days that stump was also a great sundial marking the course of the sun in a dark shadow across the waves, now to the west toward South America, now to the south and the Antarctic, and then, as the sun went down, stretching farther and farther eastward toward far-off Africa. Twice the shadow circled as Jock slowly drove the strays toward the fold. The ewes could browse during the intervals which he allowed them for rest, but Jock could not forage with them on grass and young twigs and leaves. He was forced to make short forays of his own, lying in wait for the marmots, creatures which lived and whistled among the rocks and which were difficult to catch. Sometimes, when close to the edge of the cliffs, he would follow a dangerous way along the upper ledges for the eggs or chicks of sea birds. Only his hunger made him so daring, for the ledges were narrow, and the angry parent birds struck at him with beaks and wings, rousing the whole colony with their screams. But an even greater danger than the birds was the wind, which seemed eager to fling the intruder down into the waves a thousand feet below.

Then the wind would drop, and, pursued by the birds, Jock would make his way up again to the meadows and the sheep, his hunger satisfied for a while. The little group had to travel slowly so that the wounded sheep might gather her strength. The lamb, too, was weak, for it had been only a few hours old when Jock fought off the eagle. But at last Jock brought his charges to the trail leading to the sheepfold. As they made their way down the gully, Jock was increasingly aware that something was wrong. There was no welcoming shout from Old Tom at the foot of the trail; there was no sound of bleating from sheep and lambs in the fold. In other years the flock had been kept there until the shearing was over, and then Jock had driven them back onto the mountain and returned to the settlement, leaving them to their own devices until his master sent him off again, to bring them down for dipping, or dosing with medicines, or shearing.

But this year everything was strange. Bewildered, Jock drove his three charges to the fold. It was empty. The gate stood open. There was no sign of Old Tom anywhere. He was not at the fold, he was not in the shepherd's hut, and the odour and smoke and hissing from the direction of the village were far worse than they had been when Jock had left for the mountain.

The dog was afraid to go nearer, but his training was stronger than his fear. It was his duty to find his master and to deliver to him the sheep for which he had been sent. They, too, had guessed by now at some unknown danger and huddled in one corner of the fold, their eyes staring. It was all Jock could do to get them out through the gate and started off on the path toward the settlement.

Their way led them by the potato fields, each one walled with volcanic stones. The plants were well up, green against the blackness of the soil.

The potatoes from these fields and the fish from the sea were the mainstay of men's lives here on the island.

But today the cows and oxen, usually kept carefully in the pasture at the end of the promontory, were loose in the fields, munching away at the young potato plants. And among the cattle, some of Old Tom's sheep were scattered, chewing with a sidewise twist of their narrow jaws and gazing at Jock with a pale, insolent stare.

The world had gone topsy-turvy. All the foundations of Jock's life were slipping.

And then he saw, lying across one of the stone walls, the first dead dog.

Chapter Four

JOCK STOPPED. A whimper stirred in his throat, and irresistibly he raised his muzzle and howled in mourning. Being a dog, he howled for the death of a dog, and this was a dog he knew well, a big yellow mongrel with tail curling over his back. Mike was the friend of all the village and had belonged to three boys. The middle one he had saved when the boy fell off the canning-factory pier into deep water, unnoticed by anyone but Mike. The boys had adored him. He had been with them all day and at night had slept at the foot of their big bed.

Now Mike lay, half on and half off the wall,

blasted to death by a shotgun, apparently attempting to escape from some horror of which Jock could not even guess. But shaken as Jock was, and heavy-hearted, he must go on. He could not stop here; he must find Old Tom and deliver the sheep he had been sent for.

The ewes had stopped, too, uneasy, but hardly knowing why. The death of a dog, as such, did not stir them, for dogs were the enemy. Only Jock was tolerated, as their enemy-turned-guardian, severe, but protecting. However, death was death, and they didn't like it. And they didn't like the strange smell and the sound in the air. But, responding to a bark, they went on, Jock behind them. As they topped a low hill, for the first time they could see the settlement below them on its almost unprotected harbour. At the far end the canning factory had always stood with its pier, but now the building lay under a heap of ashes and lava, and the pier ran, burned and twisted, into the sea.

The strangest thing was the new snout of a volcano which rose where the mud puddle had been, high up along the side of the mother mountain, like a horrible calf. But where the mountain was cold and silent, as it had been for centuries, this new crater was tossing smoke and ashes and rocks into the air, and from its lip a spittle of red-hot lava flowed unceasingly into the sizzling sea.

The two ewes stared, balked a little, but then ignored the new conditions and were soon grazing in the garden of a nearby cottage, where some of the sheep and cattle were already making themselves very much at home. Others were resting, complacently chewing their cud, in the cottages, which stood with their doors open to any visitor.

But, for a dog, the village was accursed. Not a human being moved along its winding street, not a voice was to be heard. Leaving the sheep, Jock ran to Old Tom's house. Here, too, the door was open, and a bullock was standing, half in and half out of the entrance. As Jock ran past him into the one big room, something rose from the bed where it had been lying. It was Missy, the cat which had belonged to Old Tom's daughter before she went away on one of the rare ships.

Clearly Missy was glad to see Jock again. She jumped down and rubbed against his side, purring and walking on her tiptoes, her tail straight in the air. Perhaps she, too, missed Old Tom and the others, but she was fat and sleek and had made herself very comfortable. On the sink shelf stood pans into which condensed milk and canned vege-

tables and meat had been emptied, but, hungry as he was, Jock had as yet no thought of food. He gave Missy a quick lap of the tongue and went out again, hunting for Old Tom in garden and tool shed — in vain. There was no sign of his master. Jock ran from house to house, whimpering and searching. Everywhere the doors stood open, everywhere the sheep and cattle and the few goats trampled the once neat gardens. Everywhere the roosters and hens walked about, hunting for grubs and scattered grain. It was a holiday for birds and beasts alike. Never had food been so plentiful. Nothing now was forbidden to them. While it lasted, all was spread out, and they had only to take.

But what of the dogs? Oh, what of the dogs? For them it was a different story. If the people had vanished quite away, the dogs were there, but the dogs were dead. Brownie, who had grown cross with old age, lay dead at the end of his chain. Two puppies lay dead in a garden, and their white mother had only reached the road before she had been dropped in her tracks. Jock's favorite friend, the spaniel Rory, lay dead by his doorstep. Everywhere the story was the same. Jock ran from one to another, shivering and whining.

At the shore, where the big fishing dories had

been kept, the dogs lay thickest, nine or ten of them together, who must have followed their masters to the boats which, like the people, had disappeared. Perhaps the men had hoped to take the dogs with them, but some order must have been given, and that order had been obeyed. Why it had been given and obeyed Jock could not guess. Were not men and dogs friends? Had they not always been so? What could Jock know of the danger of leaving hungry dogs with unguarded sheep and calves? In his world such a question had never arisen, and never could arise.

All that Jock understood was that the dogs were dead and that Old Tom was gone, gone to sea — he who had never cared for fishing but had chosen a life ashore. Old Tom and the others, the men and the women and children whom Jock had known from his earliest days — all were gone. Would they come back, come back to their torn-up gardens and dirtied cottages?

Chapter Five

FOR A LONG TIME Jock stood, looking out to sea. The sky was clouding over, but shafts of sunlight lay here and there on the water, which shone like tin, half blinding his eyes. Now and then he thought he saw something moving, far out, but either it was nothing, or a sea bird which rose again into the air, crying dismally.

At last, Jock turned and trotted slowly back toward the houses, though he had not yet given up all hope. On good days the fishermen pushed out to sea, and they returned. He had no way of understanding why everyone, down to the babies, had gone fishing, leaving dead dogs and an upside-

down world behind them, but perhaps, after all, the villagers would come back, and he would at least have a master again.

Very soon he was in the village, and now his attention was distracted by the animals about him. What was his duty? Ought he to drive the cows and sheep from the gardens? But if no one closed the gates, how could he keep them out?

Everywhere the cats watched him. Some lay on the thatched roofs and stared at him, blinking. Some lay on the doorsteps, their tails curled neatly about their paws. He saw one tabby crouch and spring at a hen feeding nearby. The hen ran off, squawking, leaving a trail of feathers behind her, but the cat did not pursue. She was not hungry and had pounced more in play than in earnest, for though she had been brought up never to harm the poultry, there were no laws anymore. The cats were enjoying their freedom. They could come and go as they wished, they could sleep where they saw fit, they could purr or yowl as they pleased. Whatever they might do, no man would shout at them, no woman would lift her broom against them. The village was theirs, and well they knew it, lounging about, smug and sleek and languid with eating.

By now, as often, the clouds had begun to darken, and suddenly the sky was black, thunder grumbled, and a leafless tree of lightning blazed overhead; then the rain began to fall.

By long habit, Jock turned in at Old Tom's gate, but now, instead of the bullock, the big red bull, Savage, had taken possession of the cottage. Usually he lived in a strong paddock of his own. It was part of the craziness of things to have Savage here, sniffing at the food on the sink and dirtying the floor, like the stupid animal he was.

This time, Jock had no doubts about what he should do. He had often helped other dogs drive bullocks and cows, and now he closed in at Savage's heels and gave a sharp and angry nip at one of them. The startled bull bellowed with surprise and rage. Very quickly, for so large a beast, he swung about, overturning a chair with a crash, and, then, horned head held low, charged out of the cottage into the wind-blown rain. Jock was no mastiff to leap at the bull's sensitive nostrils and hang there. His was in-and-out fighting, not trying to hurt the bull, but merely to drive him.

Savage, however, was red-eyed with rage, and his one instinct was to kill. Again and again he charged. He was quick on his feet, but Jock was quicker, and the increasing rain helped him. Already the wet earth of the garden was slippery under the bull's hoofs, while Jock's lighter weight and his tufted and clawed paws had the advantage. In and out he danced, snapping at Savage's legs, front and back, and always leading the furious creature toward the gate. Red bull and black sky bellowed together; lightning and dog's teeth flashed; and the rain fell like a wall, blinding the bull, while the dog was cool and determined. Charge by charge, Jock led the beast out of Old Tom's garden. Charge by charge and nip by nip, he baited him down the road. He was as skillful and as daring as any matador, and he, too, had his audience, an audience of sheep and cows, staring from the shelter of bushes or from the doors of houses and sheds, and a more fastidious audience of cats, looking out through windows.

At the end of the village, Savage had had enough. He broke into a trot and headed toward his own enclosure, with Jock barking and snapping at his heels. After a little while, the dog turned back, pleased with himself and, for a few minutes, forgetting his troubles.

Missy met him at the door and welcomed him in, wet as he was. During the first part of the battle she had taken shelter on a high shelf, but then she had stood in the doorway, watching the struggle loudly receding, and now she greeted the victor's return. Together they shared some of the food left waiting on the sink.

When they had eaten, Missy leaped onto Old Tom's bed and curled herself on the pillow. Her sleepy eyes invited Jock to take the main part of the bed, but this he could not bring himself to do.

Tired, well-fed, but heavy-hearted, he went out into the dwindling rain and took shelter in his own place, the kennel. There for a long time he lay awake, soaked through and shivering in the straw, but at last he fell asleep.

Chapter Six

JOCK stayed in the village for only a few days, until he gave up hope of Old Tom's coming back from the sea. No fisherman had ever been away for so long. By now, too, life in the village had changed, and changed for the worse. Where each cottage had opened its stores, in some the supply was running low. Here and there a cat was trespassing on another cat's property, and great spittings and clawings resulted. Missy was among those who had to forage, for Jock had eaten well. Like a savage, no dog can see ahead and plan his resources. The times offer either a feast or a famine, and Jock and Missy had feasted while the food lasted.

Now Jock must raid the other cottages, and Missy must do the same, or hunt for the rats which lived their own lives in and about the village, to which they had come long ago on the sailing ships. Missy was a better ratcatcher than she was a fighter, so she soon turned to hunting and came home, wet and bedraggled, sometimes carrying the dinner she had earned the hard way.

The cats had been lords of the place, but now they were like an army which at first takes joyous possession of a conquered city and then falls to fighting over the booty.

The bond between Jock and Missy still held, but it was weakening with every hour. Jock's kennel, with the rain drumming on its low roof, no longer seemed home, a place in which to rest until it was time to go again to move the flock on the mountain. The flock! Surely if Old Tom were here, he would want the sheep to be driven back to the mountain.

One morning it cleared. Jock looked in at the cottage door, but Missy was off hunting. He fought a brindled cat for breakfast in the storekeeper's house and stopped for a moment by what had been Rory's body. Then he made a final visit to the beach where the rains had almost wiped out the old prints of feet and dory keels. Sideways along the shingles the waves were breaking with a sharp slap; the sun was bright on a bright sea, and the volcano was tossing up rocks and debris into the air like a playful child.

Slowly Jock trotted off. He could wait no longer. As he passed the outskirts of the settlement he saw one sheep. It was the pig-headed ewe which never did what anyone expected. Today she was perfectly willing to move on ahead of him, and, in fact, of all the sheep she was, for the moment, the most docile.

The others seemed to sense that now the dog had no man's authority behind him. They dodged and doubled; the lambs broke away and went off, tails flying, followed by their baaing mothers. The old ram showed fight. But by late afternoon Jock had succeeded in penning a young ram, seven ewes and nine lambs in the fold. Here at last he could hold them by lying panting across the narrow gate.

Early next morning Jock drove his small flock up the path to the mountain, with the loss of only one sheep and a lamb, which at the last possible instant broke away from the others and rushed off as if pursued by a pack of wolves. Jock let them go, knowing that it was better to lose two than all. With six ewes, eight lambs, and the young ram, he started off into a new and masterless life. Above him lay the pastures with their hungry winds. He had known them before for a few days at a time. Now they were to be his only home.

Chapter Seven

So BEGAN the life on the mountain, the life of blowing fog and pelting showers, of winds and crying birds. There was no complete shelter any-

where. Even in the heart of a thicket, both wind and rain could find out their prey. But luckily most of the sheep had not been sheared. Someone must have called Old Tom back to the village before he had more than started his work. Almost like snails, the sheep carried their houses on their backs, and Jock's black and white silky coat was lined with a heavy padding of soft, fine hair. Sheep and sheep dog did not suffer too much from the wind and the rain and the loneliness. It was the flock's real world, the world of great distances and of the sea breaking at the foot of the cliffs.

But Jock, at least, had other troubles. Above all, he and the sheep were at odds on the subject of whether or not they should remain a flock. They were accustomed to scattering as soon as they had reached the mountain. Jock was accustomed to herding them together, ready to bring down to the fold. He wore himself out pursuing obstinate ewes, but no sooner had he brought one back than he found that two were gone. It was an unequal struggle. The sheep had the advantage of numbers. Try as he would — and he tried hard! — Jock could not be everywhere at once. With each day they grew wilder, and at last the dog could do no more than let them go as they wished. But he still tried to guard them, trotting here and there over the great slopes of the volcano, checking on a couple of ewes and their lambs, appearing like a dark ghost out of the blowing fog to stare at the young ram, and then trotting off to investigate the cause of a far-off bleating.

During his rounds, Jock had to find what food he could. After the first week or two the sea birds left their nests, and there were no more eggs or chicks to be had. Mostly he lived on the marmots, learning to be as cunning as a fox in his hiding and pouncing, but, like a fox, he often went hungry. When the berries ripened, he ate those, and once or twice caught a bird, grown careless at the same feast. But he never had enough to eat. He grew thin, and the plume of his tail no longer rose jauntily in the air, its white tip following him like a star. Now he carried it low, almost trailing, and his coat was dull and matted, and he had to rest more often.

Very soon he learned that another change had taken place on the mountain. Going to drink at the lake in the crater, which had smelled so strangely the last time, he found it completely gone. It had vanished away into the depths of the earth. Hereafter, Jock and the sheep went to the rain pools among the rocks or drank from the narrow streams which threaded the wet heights and fell in ribbons over the cliffs.

There was almost always wind on the mountain, and sometimes it could be dangerous. One morning when Jock was at the end of the island farthest from the settlement, a gale began to blow, driving the fog before it, wave upon wave. Jock, patrolling

the sheep paths along the edge of the cliffs, saw, between fog wraiths, the same headstrong ewe that he knew of old. She was grazing near the edge, leaning against the wind, too stupid to realize the danger. But Jock knew it. Crouching low to give the least possible surface to the gale, he ran between her and the abyss, barking to drive her back to safety.

But he had not counted on the young ram, unseen in the fog. At the first annoyed bleat of the obstinate ewe, something hard and hard-driven caught Jock across the ribs, knocking the wind out of him and sending him sprawling almost to the lip of the cliff. When the ram charged him again, Jock barely succeeded in dodging the lowered horns, as, with a rattle of pebbles, the ram disappeared from sight.

When he could breathe again, Jock crawled to the edge and looked over. Against all expectation, the ram had not somersaulted into the sea but had landed upon a fairly wide ledge about ten feet below the top, and lay there, evidently badly hurt, but alive.

Jock studied the ledge. His egg hunts had made him an experienced rock climber, and he saw that it would be possible for him to reach the ram

and that he might even be able to get the creature back where it belonged. As soon as a lull came in the gusts of wind, Jock dropped down to the upper end of the ledge and slowly worked his way to the ram. He might have spared himself the trouble, for it was too late to bring any help. The creature was almost dead, and all Jock could do was to watch beside him while he died.

When at last he was sure that no life was left, Jock crawled back up the ledge to the slopes above. The wind had almost blown itself out; the ewe had wandered off again, and Jock wearily sought out the lair he had found for himself among the rocks. For once, fate must have relented. Almost at its entrance, he came upon some young marmots playing and killed two of them and ate. Then he curled up, nose hidden by tail, and slept for the rest of the day and all the night.

Next morning Jock felt stronger than he had felt for some time. His first duty was to make sure that the ram was indeed dead. In the confusion of fog and wind and his own injuries, he might have been mistaken.

The day was unusually still and mild, and as far as the eye could see, the ocean lay blue and at rest. The sun shone on Jock's back as he trotted along, stopping once to drink at a little pool. This peace, coming after the turmoil of the day before, lulled Jock's senses. He was not on his guard as he came to the cliff's edge and looked downward.

But what he saw brought his hackles up and his lips back from his teeth. For there, below him on the ledge, was a man, busily skinning the ram and whistling to himself as he worked.

Chapter Eight

Jock had never expected to see a human being again, and for a moment a flood of relief swept over him, but this man was a thief and was stealing what belonged to Old Tom, and the relief was met and overwhelmed by a contrary current of rage.

At his threatening growl, the young man looked up. He was not tall but sturdy, with fair hair and gray-blue eyes.

"Hello, Jock," he said in a matter-of-fact voice, which did not sound exactly like the speech of the villagers.

Jock was taken aback by the use of his own name. He did not know this stranger, but the man knew him. A name is part of oneself. Whoever knows it establishes a bond and has power over one. Jock flinched, and for a moment the growl died away, but, as the man continued to cut up the ram, the growl began again.

The stranger went on talking in a level voice. "What are you doing here at this time of the year, Jock? You should be in the village. And why hasn't this ram been sheared? Something's wrong. Has Old Tom died and no one taken over? Is that it, Jock? And you're up here on your own, Jock, doing what you can? You don't know me, but I've seen you working the sheep at the fold, Jock, with Old Tom."

Again and again he used the names, and with each time the power strengthened, but still Jock kept his menacing position at the top of the cliff. One false step and the thief would be off the ledge. It was a dangerous place for him to be in, and both knew it.

The man went on butchering the meat, and, as he worked, he talked, and Jock listened, growling deep in his throat.

"My name's Lars," the stranger said. "Lars, short and sweet like yours, Jock, and your master's, Old Tom. I'm a Norwegian, and I was on a whaler until they put me ashore at the settlement with a bad fever, caught on the coast of South America. It was Mary who nursed me, and I learned about you at her house, Jock, and about Old Tom."

The words were like a song. They wove a spell about the listening dog. The strong, low voice, the names repeated over and over again — he could not withstand them, and again the growl died down. But every time the man changed position, the snarl jerked back into Jock's throat.

"It's good to have someone to talk to, Jock. Of course I have Sigrid, but a gull's not like a dog. The one bad thing about Black Cove is that it's lonely. I need you, Jock, and I guess you need me. You're over-thin, and your coat's a mess, old boy. Soon it will be time for me to take my salted fish round to the settlement. Then, Jock, we'll find out what's happened."

The man rose to his feet, wrapped the meat he had chosen in the ram's skin, and began moving up the ledge, keeping his gray-blue eyes on Jock's brown ones.

"So, Jock, so, boy. If Old Tom's alive he wouldn't mind. No one could find this carcass, Jock, before the birds got it. Steady, Jock, steady, boy. It's all right. I'm doing no harm. Good boy. That's right,

Jock. Steady, steady. Ah! Good boy. Now that feels a lot better. Good Jock. Let's get back from the edge, and we can make friends."

But though Jock had been hypnotized into letting Lars by, he was not yet ready to make friends. He would not allow the young man to touch him, and, at last, Lars gave up, found the pail, half filled with the berries he had been gathering, and, shouldering what he had taken of the ram, walked slowly away, not looking back.

All that day and in the days to follow, loneliness and hunger and the memory of Lars's voice speaking his name worked upon Jock, but he did not and could not give in at once, though every morning Lars came back and talked to him quietly, and, with each visit he seemed less a stranger. At last came a day when Jock followed him, and so, standing a little away from Lars's side, looked down into the one-man settlement called Black Cove, which was hereafter to be his home.

Chapter Nine

If the island was like a great volcanic stump of a tree, then Black Cove lay between two strong roots, protected from the winds. Here on the dark beach the sea came in gently, in ripples and small waves. The cove faced into the sun, and, sheltered as it was, lay green and fruitful, while in the center a narrow waterfall fell down the cliff.

There was no other such place on all that barren island. It seemed like a little Eden, hidden away. Here, even the cliffs were low. Instead of towering a thousand feet, they rose a mere fifty or sixty, and with a slant which had made it possible for Lars to build rough stone steps from ledge to

ledge, so that he could easily climb up to the pastures at any time.

As Lars came down these steps with Jock at his heels, a seagull flew up from the small beach and circled overhead, uttering scolding yelps.

Lars laughed. "Sigrid doesn't like you, Jock, but she'll get used to you. I found her fallen out of a nest, with one leg so badly hurt that I had to take most of it off and fit a wooden leg to her, like a

pirate's. She's very clever about it. Sigrid, Sigrid. Come on, girl, Jock won't hurt you," and he talked the gull to his shoulder as he had talked Jock off the mountain.

The settlement had always been fairly neat, though people had a tendency to throw this and that over their walls into the road. But Black Cove was shipshape from shore to cliff, and Lars showed Jock about as if he were a human friend.

"Here's my dory," Lars explained. "And over there are the rocks where I dry fish to take to the village. I go there about once a month to trade. I don't need much myself, but I want everything to be nice for Mary when she comes. You must know Mary, Jock. She's the prettiest and kindest girl in the village. Me, I'm just a Norwegian, but Mary's half a dozen things — and all of them good. After meeting her, I was looking for a place to settle, and one day some of the men I was fishing with put in here. I liked it from the first. No one had ever claimed it. There's only room for one family, you see. But I prefer it that way, and Mary doesn't mind. I'm hoping we can get married the next time I go to the village."

As he talked, from time to time Lars gave Sigrid a piece of crust. Her pale eyes glared, but she took each piece gently, careful not to hurt his fingers with her strong beak. Soon she had stopped her seagull grumbling, and peacefully the three continued to examine the small domain: the wavering waterfall, the stream like a glassy serpent winding between grasses and wild flowers to the shore, the little walled garden of vegetables, the orchard with its three young apple trees and a cherry tree, and, last of all, the cottage. Like the village houses, it was built of volcanic rocks, whitewashed, with a chimney and a thatched roof, but there the likeness stopped. Instead of a window on either side of a low batten door, there was one large bay window of shining glass and a door with a brass handle.

"I got them from the wreck on Johnson's Point," Lars said with satisfaction. "They came from the bridge. Wonder is the glass hadn't been smashed to bits, but it hadn't. Now come inside."

As the door opened, Sigrid flew up from Lars's shoulder and with a scream went off to her beach-combing. She was privileged, but not allowed in the house, nor did she wish to go there. Comrades they might be, but Lars had his life, and she had hers.

Inside, the house was even less like those of the

village than it was outside, for only the front part,
with its door, window, and great stone fireplace had

been man-built. The rear was a cave, whitewashed and domed, and here stood Lars's sail and rudder, oars and fishing gear, and in another place his ax and saw, hoe and spade, and a chest in which he kept his clothes.

"I made that box myself from wood that comes ashore. The current brings it sometimes, and I don't know where from. The nearest lived-on island, even, is sixteen hundred miles away, and Africa and South America are further still. But it comes. The logs and trash I dry in the sun and use for firewood. But there are ships' timbers, now and then, and sheathing. I made the chest and shelves from them, and my bed, and that table, and the chairs in the window."

Like the house, the furniture was well made, and there was even some carving on the bed's head-board, and a woolen top blanket, like the ones all the village women wove, but embroidered with a border of bright flowers.

Lars showed it to Jock. "Mary did that as a sur-prise for me. When she comes, there will always be a bouquet on the table, I think, or a dish of shells, if there are no flowers. But, what a fool I am! You are a fine listener, Jock, and it has done me good to have you to talk to. But what do you care for shells or flowers? What you need is food, and lots of it. Talk! Talk! Talk! You should nip my heels as you do a foolish sheep's, Jock, and remind me of my manners."

In no time at all, Lars had opened a can of hash and mixed it with some porridge, which stood in a covered bowl, and had placed a heaping tin on the hearth, but Jock waited to be invited to eat before at last he went toward the food and, having eaten, looked up, waving his tail slowly in thanks.

"From now on that's your dish," Lars said. "Lie down, Jock, there on the sheepskin by the coals. Yes, you may lie there," but Lars had to go and pat the sheepskin before Jock could believe that such a soft, warm place could be meant for him.

Once he understood, however, he turned about on it two or three times, like one of his wild ancestors treading down a bed in the brush, and then sank down with a long sigh of contentment.

After the troubled days on the mountain, to sleep, full-fed and warm, with a master beside him, quietly at work mending a landing net, was better than anything Jock had dreamed in his most hopeful dreams. This man was kind to him as Old Tom had never been. Here Jock lay, on a soft bed by the fire, not in the windy kennel on musty straw.

When necessary, Old Tom had given him a curt order, but young Lars talked to him, and his voice was deep and friendly. As Jock lay drowsing into sleep, a new feeling stirred in his heart. It was not the respect he had felt for the shepherd, not the sense of work, understood and shared. This was something different, something almost painful. This was love.

Chapter Ten

As the days went on, the bond between Lars and Jock strengthened. Wherever Lars went, Jock went, too, about the cove or on the mountain for berries. But these mountain excursions were troubling to him. When it came to masters, he never wavered. His choice was made, his love was given. But the sheep, ah, they were another matter. To be on the mountain, to see a ewe far off, to hear a lamb bleating for its mother, to hear and see these things and to do nothing, was very difficult for Jock.

One day when they climbed the crude stairway to the slopes, Lars took along a big pair of shears and some burlap bags.

"They aren't clippers," he said, "and I'm not a shepherd, but something's wrong with Old Tom, and it's time the ewes were sheared. If I can get a few fleeces I can make a nice wool-stuffed mattress for the bed. Mary will like that. Go fetch them in, Jock! Fetch them, boy!" And he gave a wide gesture which sent Jock off like a shot, the wind rippling down his sides.

Oh, what a day that was! It was windy, but warmer than usual. To Jock the whole world seemed to be shining. Tongue out, eyes bright, he ran here, he ran there. He was so clever that he knew there was no place in which he could pen even the smallest flock. Ewe by ewe, with perhaps a baaing lamb or two at her heels, he brought the sheep in, drove each into Lars's waiting hands, and then stood by, ready to help, as Lars threw the struggling creature and held her down, often sitting on her to keep her still, while he sheared her as best he could. This was no matter of whole fleeces, taken off like coats. The wool came away in tufts and patches, and at first there were scratches, too, but Lars learned quickly, even with no one to teach him. By the third ewe, he had got the hang of the business, and his handling of the fourth was almost professional.

But the fourth was the last, and, when she ran
off, looking half her former size and so ugly and
awkward that it was a wonder her lamb recognized

her, Lars put down the shears and stowed the wool in the bags he had brought.

"After it's soaked in the pool, I'll wash it and dry it and stuff my mattress. No more ferns for me from now on! What a good sheep dog you are, Jock — and how happy you have been today. Ah, everyone is happy when he has work to do and does it well!"

It was a few mornings later that Sigrid showed them her cave. Probably she had no intention of sharing her secret, even with Lars, but he had been feeding her, and, when she flew off, he looked after her idly. She flew behind the waterfall and did not come out on the other side.

"Now that's odd, Jock," Lars said. "I've seen her do that before. Her wooden leg makes quite a noise when she lands on a ledge, and the other gulls don't seem to like it. So she goes off by herself. But what kind of perch can she have found behind the fall? Let's go see, Jock. That's the way to answer the question."

The fall was a long one and fell free of the rock by five or six feet. Beneath it, the going was rough and slippery, and at first the sound was staggering, and the light seemed dim.

"Well, there's a ledge," said Lars, looking up, "but I don't see Sigrid. Wait! That shadow might be the entrance to a cave. This whole cove is honeycombed with them. Now how can I get up to see? I like to know what I have on my own place."

The ledge, with its line of darkness above, was not more than twenty feet up the cliff, and, when Lars began to study how he might get there, he gave a whistle of surprise. What seemed like the remains of a very narrow and zigzag trail led from cove level up toward the cave, if cave it was.

"Someone made that path," Lars said. "But who? It took more time to make than anyone from the settlement ever had to spare in Black Cove. No, you stay here like a good dog. There are handholds for me, but you couldn't make it."

For once Jock didn't obey. Where Lars went, he would go, and Lars was so busy working his own way up the cliff that he was nearly at the top before he realized that Jock was close behind him, pressed against the rock, stepping with greatest care.

"I told you not to come!" Lars exclaimed, a little angrily, but there was nothing now that he could do but go ahead. He pulled himself up on the final ledge and, reaching down, hauled Jock up after him by the snow-white scruff of his neck. At that moment, Sigrid flew out, screaming, and man and dog turned to see what she had flown out of.

Lars had been right. There was a cave behind the falls, small at its entrance but larger inside. Sigrid was gone, but the place still seemed filled with white, flying sea birds. They were everywhere, and the sunlight through the falling water, veiling the entrance, flickered across their outspread wings, so that they seemed to be alive and in motion. So real was this effect, that instinctively Lars threw up his arm to protect his face and then laughed.

"Why, they're painted on the walls, Jock," he said. "Who in this wide world painted them?"

That was a question to which he was never to find an answer. The cave was empty, and, though the paintings looked as if they might have been done only yesterday, probably they had been made long, long ago. At some time the floor had been covered with fine sand, and, at the back, in the shadows, Lars and Jock, by the light of a candle Lars took from his pocket, discovered a platform of stone. On it lay the skeleton of a man, his arms along his sides, wrapped in the remains of some sort of robe. Beside him were two spears, what was left of a carved wooden bowl, and a long, rotted staff, with a cracked and yellowed ivory gazelle for a handle.

"So," Lars said at last. "There were people here

before the settlers came, and *they* came to the island more than a hundred years ago. This was surely a chief. Did his people live on the island, or were they blown here in a storm and went away again, perhaps trying to get back to Africa? Unless we're dreaming, Jock, more than driftwood has been carried to the cove with the currents. Well, we'll touch nothing. Let him lie with his things about him, under the flying gulls, till judgment day. You'll tell no one, I know that, Jock, and neither will I, except Mary."

Chapter Eleven

AFTER finding the cave, Lars couldn't settle down until he could get to the settlement to tell Mary of this new wonder. Not waiting for a full boatload of dried fish, he was off on the first good day, and, as usual, Jock went with him.

"If Old Tom's alive, he'll want you, Jock," Lars said. "But I can't help hoping I can keep you."

So together they left Black Cove, sailing away from the beloved cottage and the sound of the waterfall. They had made a very early start, while the morning star still trembled in the sky like a drop of dew hanging on a pale green leaf. Soon, like dew, it was gone, and the sun rose over the endless heaving of the sea. Lars had chosen a day when he could count on a following wind, and now they bowled along below the mountain, with the small waves creaming at their bow and a dolphin for company.

Lars sat at the tiller with an air of suppressed excitement and happiness, and now and then spoke of Mary, eager to tell her of his discovery and hoping she would feel that this time they might marry. But once or twice, as the day went on, in a flaw of the breeze, he said perhaps a whale had been stranded somewhere on the rocks, for there was unmistakably a bad smell in the air. Jock recognized that smell which he had forgotten. It brought back his old uneasiness, and he pressed against Lars's knee, shivering.

"Good Jock!" Lars said, leaning down to pat the dog's head. "What's the trouble, old man?"

But long before they reached the village, Lars shared Jock's uneasiness. First there was the stain of smoke in the air, much less than when Jock had last seen it, but there it was.

"Something's on fire, but more than a house. Could they be burning over the pasture? It's not like that either. . . ." Lars's voice died away. Then around a point appeared the raw pink snout of the new volcano, pushing from sea level, halfway to the height of the cliffs. But still Lars did not know all that Jock knew, and he went nearly mad with anxiety. Had the village been destroyed? Were the people dead? Where was Mary? Where was his Mary?

Now they were in sight of the settlement. The canning factory was gone, but most of the cottages were there.

"But there's no smoke coming from the chimneys! Not from any of them," Lars said, and he groaned. A sudden hope came to him. "They may be camping out in the potato fields." But then he saw that the dories were gone and fell silent.

It was late in the afternoon before their own keel grated along the empty beach, and Lars jumped out to pull the heavy boat above high-water mark. Jock was at his heels, but he was like a dog that has been beaten. He circled the heap of carcasses on the sand. Sea birds and hungry cats had stripped them to bones and even the bones had been scattered.

Lars gave them one pitying glance and began to run toward the houses, with Jock close behind. In all this nightmare world, he still had his master, and, so long as he had him, he need not quite despair. The settlement had changed somewhat since Jock had last seen it. All the sheep and cattle were gone. No Savage was there to charge him, but two or three goats were visible on the shed roofs, reflectively chewing at the thatch, and several lean cocks and hens stood on the ridgepoles of the houses, warily turning their heads from side to side in endless watchfulness.

The skeleton dogs lay much where they had fallen, but the cats, the cats had changed indeed. They were lean and scarred. Some had lost part of an ear; a few were one-eyed; all bore the marks of battle. They were furtive and menacing. They skulked and they swaggered, and, like brigands, they glared at the intruding man and dog who had come to dispute with them the ownership of the village.

Probably Lars never saw them. He was running toward Mary's house, past what had once been the garden, and then went in through the open door.

"Mary!" he shouted once, though already he knew there would be no answer. She was not there, but she had left a message for him, tacked to the wall, out of reach of wind or animal. It was a letter warm with love and shaken by despair.

"The government boat with the yearly supplies

has called, just at this awful time, and they say we must all go while we have the chance. I have begged them to stop for you, but they say that it is impossible and that you are in no danger at your end of the island. I tried to run away, Lars, and hide until the others had gone, so that I would be here when you came, but Father found me and made me come back to the house. I am crying so hard that I can hardly see to write. Old Tom has just come in, more excited than I have ever seen him.

" 'Now's my chance to live with my daughter in Liverpool,' he keeps saying, over and over. But, thank God, when he asks my people what they mean to do, they answer that they're returning here, and that lightens my heart a little. The government men say that this new volcano is sure to settle down after a while, and, when it does, it will be safe for us to live here again. I'll be back with the first to come — you know that."

There was more to the letter, and, when Lars had read it over two or three times, he felt comforted. He sat down on the doorstep and looked with his blue sailor's eyes far out over the darkening sea.

At last, he spoke, and his voice had a sober cheerfulness. "Mary is well and safe, and that's what matters most," he told Jock, who was sitting close beside him. "I was afraid that she might be dead. But she is alive and promises to come back, and Mary keeps her promises. I am a patient man, and I will wait for her, if it takes years. Mary says that Old Tom will go to his daughter, and that means you and I can stay together.

"That's one thing to the good, and the other will follow, when God wills. After we have cleaned out the cottage and had food and sleep, we'll see what is to be done."

Chapter Twelve

THE NEXT MORNING was fair, with a wind to blow the smell of the new volcano out to sea. Jock could have told his master that already the thing was much less active than it had been. No rocks were tossed into the air now, and little ash darkened the steam. As for the river of red-hot lava, it had dwindled to a trickle, flowing slowly through cooling banks to the ocean which scarcely sputtered and hissed at its touch.

But to Lars, who had never suspected such a monster, it seemed bad enough. After a hasty breakfast, he made the cottage shipshape and then sat down to write Mary a letter which she would find waiting for her when she returned. It would be tacked up where hers had been. She would see it the moment she entered the door, and it would tell her all she wanted to know. Lars wrote slowly, moving his lips with every word. When he came to drawing the doves and hearts and flowers with which he decorated the margins, he worked much faster, for he was surer of his drawing than of his English spelling.

Jock sat at his feet, sharing his anxiety until the letter was finished. If Lars looked up and asked him, "Has 'married' two r's or one, Jock?" he wagged the plume of his tail slowly along the floor. At last it was finished.

"There," said Lars, with relief. "Now for something easier." He spent most of the morning unloading the cargo of salt fish into one of the fish houses near the water and, when he had finished, left neither door nor window open.

"That's my bank account," he explained. "As for the cats, they can catch rats. Now that's all's unloaded, we'll eat and then go shopping on credit."

The village post-office-and-store was in a woodshed, somewhat larger than the others, and here the door had been left shut, but not locked, for there was not a lock on the whole island. Jock followed Lars in. There were many shelves with a variety of necessities on them: cans and cartons of food, rolls of cloth, pots, pans, kitchen knives, a few plates, and, against one wall, fishing gear. The stock was small compared to that of a store on the mainland, and yet everything was here that the islanders needed.

Lars chose carefully, making two lists of what he took, one to leave for Ernest, the storekeeper, and one for himself. He kept adding things which he thought Mary would like. When at last he came out with Jock at his heels, he made a wide gesture.

"Run along, boy! You can't help carry stuff down to the boat. I'll need you later, but not now."

Jock understood the gesture, if not the words. It was true that there were places to which he wanted to go. First he went to Old Tom's cottage, where his kennel stood, still furnished with the hay his own body had pressed flat. He sniffed at it. No one had been there since he left, cat or rat, but the hay was sour with the dampness.

When Jock trotted through the door of the house, Missy was in her favourite place on the bed, lying against the pillow. She hadn't heard him coming and woke with a start, bristling and spitting. Then she recognized him and gave a little meow of welcome as she jumped to the floor and walked to meet him. But the last weeks had deepened her distrust. She was a good hunter and seemed to have had enough food, but in these days it was every cat for herself. Old friends had turned into new enemies.

So Missy spun about suddenly, before she had reached Jock, and shot under the bed, where she remained. No barks or whines could coax her out of hiding, and at last Jock trotted off and left her.

He wanted to see the sheep. Everywhere about the village were the gaunt and unfriendly cats, with their watchful eyes. He even found a few cats in the fields. At sight of him they ran, close to the ground, apparently without legs, like so many gliding snakes.

He trotted on, puzzled but indifferent. Missy was another matter. Missy was his cat. Some day, when he had more time, he would make friends with her again. Now he must see the sheep and get back to Lars.

He found only a few of the flock, mostly in the pasture, for the potato plants had long ago been pulled up and eaten. The old ram was there and charged him, as did Savage, and both he dodged, while the cows and ewes looked on, chewing their cud as they watched. Did the sheep remember him? He had no way of telling. The second young ram and a few of the other sheep were gone; probably they had joined the others on the mountain as forage in the fields grew scarce.

The old ram gave a final charge, and Jock jumped over the black stone pasture wall, not from any fear, but because it was time to get back to Lars. He returned to the settlement at an easy gallop, and it was as well that he hurried, for Lars was whistling for him.

He had a couple of empty cartons beside him and held a landing net in one hand. "Now we're going to see if we can get a few hens and a rooster or two before the cats finish up the last of them," he told Jock. "See that fellow on the roof? You get on the other side and bark to attract his attention, while I go after him with the net."

It was not an easy business. The chickens were wary from living with one eye always on the cats. But both Lars and Jock were swift and skillful, and they enjoyed the hunt. At the end of two hours they had bagged four lean hens and two bedraggled roosters and had popped them, squawking, into

the boxes, with a few handfuls of corn to comfort them when their fears should subside a little.

Next Lars pointed out a goat and her half-grown kid.

"We'll take these now. Mary will like having fresh milk, and, later, I'll bring a couple of sheep down from the pasture, so she can have wool when she needs it. That ought to please you, Jock." Jock was pleased already. This was work he understood completely, though he had never tried to drive a goat and was surprised by this one's way of rearing and striking sideways at him with her sharp horns. Once she caught him in the ribs and knocked the wind out of him, but her victory was short. It didn't take him long to pen her in the angle of a house and shed, and then Lars got a rope over her horns and, with Jock nipping at her heels, pulled her down to the boat, where he lifted her in and tied her to a thwart.

"There, Gerda, old girl, you'll like Black Cove. Wait and see. Now here's your kid for company. Don't worry about him. He's tied, too, so he won't fall overboard. It's late to be starting, but the tide's right, and the sooner we start, the sooner we'll be there."

At a word, Jock jumped in, and Lars pushed the boat down the beach to a chorus of squawks and cackles and big bleats and little bleats. But when the sail was hoisted and the boat was cradled among the waves, the passengers grew silent, and Lars, too, sat silent at the tiller. The afternoon wore away to a clear night as, one by one, cluster by cluster the stars swung out of the sea. To the west, the mountain loomed up blacker than the night, and the wind, that great singer of the South Atlantic, was only humming now under its breath, lonely as ever, but for the moment half asleep, and somewhere the seagulls slept, too, their wild hearts at rest and their voices stilled.

All night the boat tacked back and forth and, in the dawn, Lars and Jock rounded the point into Black Cove. The sun's disk was half above the waves, and the first rosy light lay along the waterfall and on the whitewashed walls of the cottage. Suddenly white wings bent to them and it was Sigrid, welcoming them home.

Gerda lifted her head and looked toward the shore and bleated, smelling so much grass. A rooster crowed, and his voice, smothered in cardboard, was loud and triumphant, and Jock's tail waved, without his even knowing it. Unable to sit still another moment, he jumped up and stood with his white forepaws on the gunwale and barked and barked for joy as the boat drew near the shore.